Favorite Fairy Tales

TOLD IN NORWAY

Favorite Fairy Tales

TOLD IN NORWAY

Retold from Norse Folklore

by Virginia Haviland

Illustrated by Anita Riggio

A Beech Tree Paperback Book 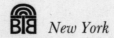 *New York*

First Beech Tree Edition, 1996, published by arrangement with Little, Brown and Co.
Printed in the United States of America

10 9 8 7 6 5 4 3 2 1

These stories have been adapted from the 1859 translation by Sir George Webb Dasent of Norwegian folk tales gathered by Peter Christian Asbjornsen and Jorgen E. Moe.

Library of Congress Cataloging-in-Publication Data

Haviland, Virginia, 1911–1988
        Favorite fairy tales told in Norway / retold by Virginia Haviland ; illustrated by Anita Riggio.
        p.   cm.
        Contents: The princess on the glass hill — Why the sea is salt —
The three billy goats Gruff — Taper Tom — Why the bear is stumpy-tailed —
The lad and the north wind — Boots and the troll.
        ISBN 0-688-12607-3 (pbk.)
        1. Fairy tales — Norway.   [1. Fairy tales.   2. Folklore — Norway.]
I. Title.
PZ8. H295 Favn 1996
[398.21'09481]—dc20   94–1503
                                                                            CIP
                                                                            AC

Minor editorial and style changes have been made in the stories for these new editions.

Contents

Favorite Fairy Tales

TOLD IN NORWAY

The Princess
on the Glass Hill

ONCE UPON A TIME a man had a meadow
high on a hillside. In the meadow was
a barn, which the man had built to keep
his hay in.

Now, there had not been much hay in that
barn for the last year or two. Every Saint John's
Night, when the grass stood greenest and deepest, the meadow was eaten down to the very
ground by morning. It was just as if a whole herd
of sheep had been feeding on it overnight.

At last the man grew weary of losing his crop of hay. He told his three sons (the youngest was nicknamed Cinderlad) that when Saint John's Night came, one of them must go and sleep in the barn in the meadow. His grass must not be eaten, root and blade, this year, as it had been the last two years. Whoever went must keep a sharp lookout. That was what their father said.

Well, the oldest son was ready to go and watch the meadow. Trust him to look after the grass! When evening came, he set off to the barn and lay down to sleep. A little later there came such a clatter, and such an earthquake, that walls and roof shook and groaned and creaked. Up jumped the lad and took to his heels as fast as ever he could. And he dared not look around once until he reached home. As for the hay—why, it was eaten this year just as it had been before.

★ ★ ★

The next Saint John's Night, the man said again it would never do to lose all the grass this way. One of his sons must go off to watch it, and watch it well, too.

Now the next oldest son was ready to try his luck. Off he went and lay down to sleep in the barn as his brother had done before him. In the night there came such a rumbling and quaking of the earth that it was worse even than on the last Saint John's Night. When the lad heard it, he was so frightened that he took to his heels as though he were running a race.

★ ★ ★

Next year it was Cinderlad's turn. But when he made ready to go, the other two began to laugh and to make fun of him, saying, "You're just the man to watch the hay, you are! You, who have done nothing all your life but sit in the ashes and toast yourself by the fire!"

Cinderlad did not care a wit about their chattering. As evening came, he stumped up the hillside to the field. He went inside the barn and lay down. But in about an hour's time the barn began to groan and creak. It was dreadful to hear.

"Well," said he to himself, "if it isn't worse than this, I can stand it."

A little while after came another creak and an earthquake, so that the straw litter in the barn flew about the lad's ears.

"Oh," said Cinderlad to himself, "if it isn't worse than this, I dare say I can stand it."

Just then came a third rumbling, and a third earthquake, so that the lad thought walls and roof were coming down on his head. But it passed off, and all was still as death about him.

It'll come again, I'll be bound, thought Cinderlad. But no, it didn't come again. Quiet it was, and quiet it stayed.

After Cinderlad had lain a little while, he heard a noise as if a horse were standing just outside the barn door, cropping the grass. He stole to the door and peeped through a hole. There stood a horse feeding away. So big and fat and grand a horse Cinderlad had never set eyes on. By its side on the grass lay a saddle and bridle and a full set of armor for a knight. It was all of brass, so bright that the light gleamed from it.

"Ho, ho!" said the lad to himself. "It's you, is it, that eats up our hay? I'll soon stop that. Just see if I don't."

Out of his tinderbox he took the bit of steel he used for striking sparks to make fire and threw it over the horse. Then the horse had no power to stir from the spot. In fact, the horse became so tame that the lad could do with it what he liked. He got on its back and rode off to a place which no one knew of, and there he left the horse.

When Cinderlad got home, his brothers laughed and asked how he had fared.

"Well," said Cinderlad, "all I can say is, I lay in the barn till the sun rose, and neither saw nor heard anything. I can't think what there was in the barn to make you both so afraid."

"A pretty story," said his brothers. "But we'll soon see how you have watched the meadow."

Off they went. When they reached the meadow, there stood the grass as deep and thick as it had been the day before.

★ ★ ★

Well, the next Saint John's Night it was the same story over again. Neither of the older brothers dared to go to the outlying field to watch the crop.

But Cinderlad was brave enough to go, and everything happened just as it had happened the year before. First a clatter and an earthquake, then a greater clatter and another earthquake. And so on a third time. Only this year the earthquakes were much worse than the year before.

Then all at once everything was as still as death. The lad heard something cropping the grass outside the barn. He stole to the door and peeped through a hole. What do you think he saw? Why, another horse chewing and chomping with might and main! It was far finer and fatter than the one who had come the year before. It had a saddle on its back and a bridle on its neck. A full suit of mail for a knight lay by its side, all of silver, as grand as you would wish to see.

"Ho, ho!" said Cinderlad to himself. "It's you that gobbles up our hay, is it? I'll soon stop that." With that he took the steel out of his tinderbox and threw it over the horse's head. The horse stood as still as a lamb. Well, the lad rode this horse, too, to the hiding place where he kept the other one. After that he went home.

"I suppose you'll tell us," said his brother, "there's a fine crop this year, too, up in the hayfield."

"Well, so there is," said Cinderlad. Off ran the others to see, and there stood the grass thick and deep, as it was the year before. But they didn't give him softer words for all that.

★ ★ ★

Now, when the third Saint John's Night came, the two older brothers were still not brave enough to lie out in the barn and watch the grass. They had been too frightened.

But Cinderlad dared to go. The very same thing happened this time. Three earthquakes came, one after the other; each was worse than the one before. And when the last came, the lad danced about with the shock, from one barn wall to the other. After that, all at once, it was still as death.

Now when Cinderlad had lain a little while, he heard something tugging away at the grass outside the barn, so he stole again to the door and peeped out, and there stood a horse. It was far, far bigger and fatter than the two he had taken before. It had a saddle on its back and a bridle on its neck. A full suit of mail for a knight lay by its side, all of gold, and more splendid than anything you ever saw.

"Ho, ho!" said the lad to himself. "It's you, is it, that comes here eating up our hay? I'll soon stop that." He caught up his steel and threw it over the horse's neck, and in a moment the horse stood as if it were nailed to the ground. Cinderlad could do with it as he pleased. He rode off to the hiding place where he kept the other two.

When Cinderlad got home, his two brothers

made fun of him as they had done before. They said they could see he had watched the grass well, for he looked as if he were walking in his sleep.

They said many other cruel things, too, but Cinderlad paid no attention. He asked them only to go and see for themselves. They found the grass standing as fine and deep this time as it had been twice before.

★ ★ ★

Now, you must know that the King of this country had a daughter, whom he would give only to the man who could ride up over the hill of glass. This was a high, high hill—all of glass, as smooth and slippery as ice—close by the King's palace. Upon the tiptop of the hill the King's daughter was to sit, with three golden apples in her lap. The man who could ride up and carry off the three golden apples would win half the kingdom and the Princess for his wife.

The King had posted a notice on all the church doors in his realm, and had given it out in many other kingdoms besides.

The Princess was so beautiful that all who set eyes on her fell in love with her whether they wanted to or not. I needn't tell you how all the princes and knights who heard of the King's offer were eager to win her along with half the kingdom. From all parts of the world they came riding on high prancing horses, and they were clad in the grandest clothes. Every one of them had made up his mind that he alone was to win the Princess.

When the day of trial came, there was such a crowd of princes and knights at the foot of the glass hill that it made your head whirl to look at them. Everyone in the country who could so much as crawl was off to the hill, too. They were all eager to see the man who was to win the Princess.

Cinderlad's two older brothers set off with the rest. But as for Cinderlad, they said plainly that he was not to go with them. If they should be seen with such a dirty creature, all covered with smut from cleaning their shoes and sifting cinders in the ash-hole, folk would make fun of them.

"Very well," said Cinderlad. "It's all one to me. I can go alone, and stand or fall by myself."

Now when the two brothers came to the hill of glass, the knights and princes were hard at it, riding their horses till they were all in a foam. But it was no good. As soon as the horses set foot on the hill, they slipped right down. There wasn't one who could get even a horse's length up the slope. And no wonder, for the hill was as smooth as a sheet of glass and as steep as a house wall.

But all were eager to have the Princess and half the kingdom. So they rode and slipped and rode—and still it was the same story over again.

At last all their horses were so weary they could scarcely lift a hoof and in such a sweat that the lather dripped from them. The knights had to give up trying.

The King was thinking that he would proclaim a new trial for the next day, to see if anyone would have better luck, when all at once a knight came riding up on so gallant a steed that no one had ever seen the like of it in his born days. The knight had mail of brass, and the horse had a brass bit in his mouth so bright that the sunbeams shone from it.

All the others called out to him that he might just as well spare himself the trouble of trying to ride up that hill. It would lead to no good. But he gave no heed to them. He headed his horse up the hill and climbed it like nothing for a third of the way. But when he was this far along, he turned his horse around and rode down again. The Princess thought she had never seen so fine a knight. While he was riding, she sat and said to herself, "I wish to Heaven he might come up the hill and go down the other side!"

When she saw him turning back, she threw down one of the apples. It rolled after him into his shoe. As soon as he reached the bottom of the hill he rode off so fast that no one could tell what had become of him.

That evening all the knights and princes were to go before the King so that the one who had ridden up the hill might show the apple which the Princess had thrown. One after the other they all came, but not a man could show the apple.

At evening Cinderlad's brothers came home, too, and had a long story to tell about the riding up the hill.

"First of all," they said, "there was not one of the riders who could get even one step up the hill. But at last came a knight who had a suit of brass mail and a brass bridle and saddle—all so bright that the sun shone from them a mile off. There was a man to ride! He rode a third of the way up the hill of glass. He could easily have ridden the whole way up, but he turned round and rode down, maybe thinking that was enough for once."

"I should so like to have seen him," said Cinderlad, who was sitting by the fire.

"Oh," said the brothers, "you would, would you? You look fit to keep company with such high lords—you, sitting there in the ashes!"

★ ★ ★

The next day the brothers were all for setting off again. Cinderlad begged them this time, too, to let him go with them and see the riding. But no, they wouldn't have him at any price.

"Well, well," said Cinderlad, "if I go at all, I must go by myself. I'm not afraid."

When the brothers reached the hill of glass, all the princes and knights were beginning to ride again. They had taken care to shoe their horses sharp this time. But it was no good— they rode and slipped, and slipped and rode, just as they had done the day before. There was not one who could get even a horse's length up the hill. And when they had worn out their horses, they were all forced to give it up.

The King thought he might as well proclaim that the riding should take place the next day for the last time, just to give them one chance more. But then it came across his mind that he might as well wait a little while longer to see if the knight in brass mail would come again.

All at once someone came riding on a steed that looked far, far braver and finer than the one which the knight in brass had ridden. This knight wore silver mail, and his horse had a silver saddle and bridle, all so bright that the sunbeams gleamed and glanced from them far away.

The others shouted out to him again, saying he might as well hold and not try to ride up the hill, for all his trouble would be wasted. But the knight paid no heed to them. He rode straight at the hill and right up till he had gone two thirds of the way. Then he wheeled his horse around and rode down again.

To tell the truth, the Princess liked him even better than the knight in brass. She sat and wished he might be able to come right up to the top and down the other side. When she saw him turning back, she threw the second apple after him, and it rolled down and fell into his shoe. But as soon as he came down from the hill of glass, he rode off so fast that no one could see what became of him.

That evening, again, everyone was to go before the King and the Princess, so that the one who had the golden apple might show it. In they went, one after the other—but no one had an apple.

The two brothers again went home and told how things had gone, how every knight and prince had tried the hill, and none could ride on it.

"But last of all," they said, "came a knight in a silver suit, and his horse had a silver saddle and a silver bridle. There was a man to ride! He rode two thirds of the way up the hill, but then he turned back. He was a fine fellow! The Princess threw her second golden apple to him."

"Oh," said Cinderlad, "I should so like to have seen him, too! That I should."

"A pretty story," they said. "Perhaps you think his coat of mail was as bright as the ashes you are always poking about and sifting."

★ ★ ★

The third day everything happened as it had twice before. Cinderlad begged to go and see the riding, but his brothers would not hear of it.

When the brothers reached the hill, they found again that no one could climb so much as a horse's length up the glass. They all waited now for the knight in silver mail to appear, but they neither saw nor heard of him. At last, however, a rider came near on a steed so grand that no one had ever seen his match. This knight wore a suit of golden mail, and his horse wore a golden saddle and a golden bridle so bright that the sunbeams gleamed from them a mile away. The other knights and princes could not warn him against trying his luck, for they were struck dumb by his gallantry.

He rode right at the hill, and up he went like nothing at all, so that the Princess did not even have time to wish that he might ride the whole way. And as soon as he reached the top, he took

the third golden apple from the Princess's lap. Then he turned his horse around and rode down again. Off he went at full speed, and out of sight in a flash.

When the brothers got home that evening, you may fancy that they had a long story to tell. They had a great deal to say about that knight in golden mail.

"There was a man to ride!" they said. "Another knight so grand isn't to be found in this wide, wide world."

"Oh," said Cinderlad, "I should so like to have seen him!"

"Ah," said his brothers, "his mail shone far brighter than the coals you are always poking."

★ ★ ★

Next day all the knights and princes were to pass before the King and Princess so that the one who had the golden apple might bring it forth. One after another they came, first the princes, then the knights. No one of them could show the golden apple.

"Well," said the King, "someone must have it, for we all saw with our own eyes how a man rode up and carried it off." He then commanded that everyone who was in the kingdom should come to the palace so that the one who had the golden apple could show it.

Well, they came, one after another, but no one had the golden apple.

Cinderlad's two brothers came last of all. The King asked them if there was anyone in the kingdom who had not come.

"Oh, yes," said they. "We have a brother, but *he* never carried off the golden apple! He hasn't stirred out of his ashes on any of the three days."

"Never mind that," said the King. "He may as well come to the palace like the rest."

So Cinderlad had to go to the palace.

"How now," asked the King, "do you have the golden apple? Speak out!"

"Yes, I have," said Cinderlad. "Here is the first, and here is the second, and here is the third, too."

With that, he pulled all three golden apples out of his pocket. At the same time he threw off his sooty rags and stood before them in his gleaming golden mail.

"Well, now," cried the King. "You who could ride up the glass hill shall indeed have my daughter, and half my kingdom, too, for you have fairly won them."

Everyone prepared for the wedding. There was great merrymaking at the bridal feast, as you may imagine. They were all merry, even though they could not all ride up the glass hill. And if they have not left off their merrymaking yet—why, they are probably still at it.

Why the Sea Is Salt

ONCE UPON A TIME—but it was a long, long time ago—there were two brothers. One of them was rich and one was poor.

On Christmas Eve, the poor one had not so much as a crumb in the house, either of meat or of bread. So he went to his brother to ask him for something with which to keep Christmas. It was not the first time he had called upon his rich brother for help, and since the rich one was stingy, the poor brother was not made very welcome.

The rich brother said, "If you will go away and never come back, I'll give you a whole side of bacon."

The poor brother, full of thanks, agreed to this.

"Well, here is the bacon," said the rich brother. "Now go straight away to the Land of Hunger."

The poor brother took the bacon and set off. He walked the whole day, and at dusk he came to a place where he saw a very bright light.

"Maybe this is the place," said he and turned aside. The first person he saw was an old, old man with a long white beard who was chopping wood for the Christmas fire.

"Good evening," said the man with the bacon.

"The same to you. Where are you going so late in the day?" asked the man.

"Oh, I'm going to the Land of Hunger—if only I can find the right way."

"Well, you are not far wrong, for this is that land," said the old man. "When you go inside, everyone there will want to buy your bacon, for meat is scarce here. But mind you, don't sell it unless you get for it the hand mill which stands behind the door. When you come out again, I'll teach you how to handle the mill. You will be able to make it grind almost anything."

The man with the bacon thanked the other for his good advice. Then he gave a great knock at the door.

When he had entered, everything happened just as the old man had said it would. Everyone came swarming up to him like ants around an anthill. Each one tried to outbid the other for the bacon.

"Well," said the man, "by rights it is my wife and I who should have this bacon for Christmas dinner. However, since you have all set your hearts on it, I suppose I must let you have it. But if I do sell it, I must have in exchange that mill behind the door."

At first they wouldn't hear of such a bargain. They argued and haggled with the man. But he stuck to his bargain, and at last they had to part with the mill.

The man now carried the mill out into the yard and asked the old woodcutter how to handle it. As soon as the old man had showed him how to make it grind, he thanked him, and hurried off home as fast as he could. But the clock had struck twelve on this Christmas Eve before he reached his own door.

"Wherever in the world have you been?" complained his wife. "Here I have sat hour after hour waiting and watching, without so much as two sticks to lay together under the Christmas broth."

"Well," said the man, "I couldn't get back earlier because I had to go a long way—first for one thing, and then for another. But now you shall see what you shall see!"

Carefully he set the mill on the table. First of all, he ordered it to grind lights. Next he asked for a tablecloth, then for meat, then ale—and so on till he and his wife had every kind of thing to help them celebrate Christmas. He had only to speak the word, and the mill would grind out anything he asked for. His wife stood by, blessing her stars. She kept on asking where he had gotten this wonderful mill, but he wouldn't tell her.

"It's all one where I got it. You can see the mill is a good one. That's enough."

The man ground meat and drink and sweets enough to last till Twelfth Day. On the Third

Day he asked all his friends and kin to his house and gave a great feast.

When the rich brother arrived and saw all that was on the table and all that was stored in the larder, he grew spiteful and wild. He couldn't bear it that his brother should have anything. It made him shout, "It was only on Christmas Eve that my brother was so poor he came and begged for a morsel of food! Now he gives a feast as if he were a count or a king!"

The rich man demanded of his brother, "How did you get all this wealth?"

"From behind the door," answered the new owner of the mill. He did not intend to give away his secret. But later on in the evening, when he was quite merry, he could keep his secret no longer. He brought out the mill and said, "There, you see what has given me all this wealth." And he made the mill grind all kinds of things.

When the rich brother beheld this, his heart was set on having the mill. And he got it, after much coaxing. But he had to pay three hundred dollars, and leave the mill with his brother until hay harvest. His brother thought that if he kept it until then, he could make it grind meat and drink to last for years.

You may know that the mill did not grow rusty for lack of work to do.

When hay harvest came around, the rich brother got the mill, but the other took care not to teach him how to handle it.

It was evening when the rich brother took the mill home. Next morning he told his wife to go out into the field and toss hay. He would stay at home and get the dinner ready.

When dinnertime drew near, he put the mill on the kitchen table and ordered, "Grind herrings and broth, and grind them good and fast."

The mill began at once to grind the herrings and broth. First, they filled every dish in the house, then all the big tubs, and then they flowed all over the kitchen floor.

Madly, the man twisted and twirled at the mill to get it to stop. But for all his twisting and fingering, the mill went on grinding.

In a little while the broth rose so high that the man was about to drown. He managed to throw open the kitchen door and run into the parlor. Soon the mill had ground the parlor full, too, and it was at the risk of his life that the man reached the door through the stream of broth.

When he had managed to pull the door open, he ran out and off down the road. A stream of herrings and broth poured out at his heels, roaring like a waterfall over the whole farm.

His wife, who was still in the field tossing hay, began to think it a long time to dinner. At last she said, "Well, even though the master hasn't called us home, we may as well go. Maybe he finds it hard work to boil the broth and will be glad of my help."

The men were willing enough to go. But just as they had climbed a little way up the hill, what should they meet but herrings and broth, all running, and dashing, and splashing together in a stream? The master himself was running ahead for his very life.

As he passed the workers, he bawled out, "If only each of you could drink with a hundred throats! Take care you are not drowned in the broth."

Away he went, as fast as he could, to his brother's house, and begged him to take back the mill at once.

"If it grinds only one hour more, the whole parish will be swallowed up by herrings and broth."

But his brother wouldn't hear of taking it back until the other paid him three hundred dollars more.

So now the poor brother had both the money and the mill.

It wasn't long before he set up a farmhouse far finer than the one in which his brother lived. With the mill he ground so much gold that he covered the house with it.

Since the farm lay by the seaside, the golden house gleamed and glistened far away to ships at sea. All who sailed by came ashore to see the rich man in his golden house and the wonderful mill. The fame of the mill spread far and wide till there was nobody who hadn't heard tell of it.

One day a skipper sailed in to see the mill. The first thing he asked was whether it could grind salt.

"Grind salt!" said the owner. "I should think it could. It can grind anything."

When the skipper heard that, he said he must have the mill, no matter what it cost. If he had it, he thought he would no longer have to take long voyages across stormy seas for a cargo of salt.

At first the man wouldn't hear of parting with his mill. But the skipper begged so hard that at last he let him have it. However, the skipper had to pay a great deal of money for it.

When the skipper had the mill on his back, he went off with it at once. He was afraid the man would change his mind, so he took no time to ask how to handle the mill. He got on board his ship as fast as he could, and set sail.

When the skipper had sailed a good way off, he brought the mill up on deck and said, "Grind salt, and grind both good and fast."

Well, the mill began to grind salt so that it poured out like water.

When the skipper had filled the ship, he wished to stop the mill. But whichever way he turned it, and however much he tried, it was no good. The mill kept grinding on, and the heap of salt grew higher and higher. At last it sank the ship.

Now the mill lies at the bottom of the sea. It grinds away still this very day, and that is why the sea is salt.

The Three Billy Goats Gruff

ONCE UPON A TIME there were three billy goats who were going up the hillside to make themselves fat. The name of all three was Gruff.

On the way up, they had to cross a bridge over a stream. Under the bridge lived a great ugly Troll with eyes as big as saucers and a nose as long as a poker.

First of all over the bridge came the youngest billy goat Gruff.

Trip trap! Trip trap! went the bridge.

"WHO'S THAT TRIPPING OVER MY BRIDGE?" roared the Troll.

"Oh, it is only I, the tiniest billy goat Gruff. I'm going up to the hillside to make myself fat," said the billy goat—with such a small voice!

"NOW I'M COMING TO GOBBLE YOU UP," said the Troll.

"Oh, no, pray don't take *me*. I'm too little, that I am," said the billy goat. "Wait a bit till the second billy goat Gruff comes. He's much bigger."

"WELL, BE OFF WITH YOU," said the Troll.

A little later up came the second billy goat Gruff to cross the bridge.

Trip trap! Trip trap! Trip trap! went the bridge.

"WHO'S THAT TRIPPING OVER MY BRIDGE?" roared the Troll.

"Oh, it's the second billy goat Gruff, and I'm going up to the hillside to make myself fat," said the billy goat. His voice was not so small, either.

"NOW I'M COMING TO GOBBLE YOU UP," said the Troll.

"Oh, no, don't take *me*. Wait a little till the big billy goat Gruff comes. He's much bigger."

Just then up came the big billy goat Gruff.

Trip trap! Trip trap! Trip trap! Trip trap! went the bridge. This billy goat was so heavy that the bridge creaked and groaned under him.

"WHO'S THAT TRAMPING OVER MY BRIDGE?" roared the Troll.

"IT'S I! THE BIG BILLY GOAT GRUFF," said the billy goat. He had an ugly hoarse voice of his own.

"NOW I'M COMING TO GOBBLE YOU UP," roared the Troll.

WELL, COME ALONG! I'VE GOT
  TWO SPEARS,
AND I'LL POKE YOUR EYEBALLS
  OUT AT YOUR EARS.
I'VE GOT BESIDES TWO GREAT
  BIG STONES,
AND I'LL CRUSH YOU TO BITS,
  BODY AND BONES.

That was what the big billy goat said. He flew at the Troll and poked his eyes out with his horns. He crushed him to bits, body and bones, and tossed him out into the stream. Then he went up to the hillside. There the billy goats got so fat they were scarcely able to walk home again. If the fat hasn't fallen off them—why, they're still fat! And so...

Snip, snap, snout,
This tale's told out.

Taper Tom

ONCE ON A TIME there lived a King who had a beautiful daughter. She was so lovely that her looks were talked about near and far. But she was so sad and serious that she could never be made to laugh. And besides, she was so high-and-mighty that she said "No" to all who wooed her. She would have none of them, were they ever so grand. Lords and princes, it was all the same.

The King had long ago tired of this, for he thought she should marry, like the rest of the world. There was no good in waiting—she was quite old enough. Nor would she become any richer.

So, the King sent out word that anyone who could get his daughter to laugh should have her for his wife, and half the kingdom, too. But if anyone tried to make her laugh and could not, he was to have a beating.

Sure it was that there were many sore backs in the kingdom, for suitors came from north and south, east and west, thinking it would be nothing at all to make a King's daughter laugh.

But for all their gay tricks and capers, there sat the Princess, just as sad and serious as she had been before.

★ ★ ★

Near the palace lived a man who had
sons. They, too, had heard that the King
said the man who could make the Pri
laugh was to have her for his wife, and hal
kingdom, too.

The oldest was for setting off first. So away
strode. When he came to the King's palace, h
told the King he would be glad to try to make
the Princess laugh.

"All very well, my man," said the King, "but
it's sure to be no good. Many have been here
and tried, but my daughter is so sorrowful—it's
no use."

The lad still thought he wanted to try. It could
not be such a very hard thing for him to get the
Princess to laugh! Many people had laughed at
him when he enlisted to be a soldier and learned
to drill.

Off he went now through the courtyard to the
Princess's window, and he began to practice his

drill. But it was no good. The Princess was just as sad and serious as before. She did not so much as smile at him once. So they took him and beat him and sent him home again.

He had hardly got home before his second brother wanted to set off. This one was a schoolmaster, and a funny figure. He was lopsided, with one leg shorter than the other. One moment he was as short as a boy, and in another, when he stood on his long leg, he was as tall as a Troll. Besides being odd this way, he could preach with a powerful voice.

When he came to the King's palace and said he wished to make the Princess laugh, the King thought it might not be so unlikely after all. "But Heaven help you," he said, "if you don't make her laugh. We are beating harder and harder for every one that fails."

The schoolmaster strode off to the Princess's window and preached as loud as seven parsons

together. The King laughed so loud, he was forced to hold on to the posts in the gallery. The Princess was just going to put a smile on her lips when all at once she turned as sad and serious as ever. So it fared no better with the schoolmaster than with the soldier. They took him and beat him and sent him home again.

Now the youngest brother, who was called Taper Tom, was all for setting out. But his brothers laughed and jeered at him and showed him their sore backs. His father would not let him go, either. He said it could be of no use. Was it not true that he neither knew anything nor could do anything? There he sat in the chimney corner like a cat, grubbing in the ashes and splitting fir tapers for lights. That was why they called him Taper Tom. But Taper Tom would not give in, and at last they got tired of his begging. He, too, was to go to the King's palace and try his luck.

When he got there he did not say he wished to try to make the Princess laugh, but asked if he could get work. No, they said, they had no place for him. But Taper Tom would not give up. They must want someone, he said, to carry wood and water for the kitchen maid. At last the King thought it might very well be, for he, too, got tired of Tom's insisting. In the end Taper Tom stayed to carry wood and water for the kitchen maid.

One day, when he was going to fetch water from the brook, he saw a big fish. It was lying under an old stump, where the water had eaten into the bank. So softly did Taper Tom put his bucket under the fish that he was able to catch it.

As he was going home to the palace he met an old woman leading a golden goose by a string.

"Good day, Goody," said Taper Tom. "That's an elegant bird you have there. What fine feathers it wears! If I only had such feathers, I might leave off splitting fir tapers."

The goody was just as pleased with the fish Tom had in his bucket. She said that if he would give her the fish, she would give him the golden goose. It was a remarkable goose. When anyone touched it, if Tom only said, "Hang on, if you care to come with us," the person would be stuck fast to the goose.

Yes! Taper Tom was willing enough to make this exchange.

"A bird is as good as a fish, any day," he said to himself. "And if it's such a bird as you say, I can use it as a fishhook."

Now, he hadn't gone far before he met another old woman. As soon as she saw the lovely golden goose, she was all for patting it. She begged Tom to let her stroke his lovely golden goose.

"It's fine with me," said Taper Tom. "But mind you don't pluck out any of its feathers."

Just as she stroked the goose, he said, "Hang on, if you care to come with us!"

The goody pulled and tore, but she was forced to hang on, whether she wanted to or not. Taper Tom walked on ahead, as though he alone were with the golden goose.

When he had gone a bit farther, he met a man who was angry with the goody for a trick she had played on him. When he saw how fast she was stuck to the goose, he thought he would be quite safe in giving her a kick with his foot.

"Hang on, if you care to come with us!" called out Tom, and the man had to limp along on one leg, whether he wanted to or not. When he jibbed and jibed and tried to break loose, it got even worse for him, for he almost fell flat on his back with every step he took.

They went on a good bit until they were near the King's palace. There they met the King's smith, who was going to the smithy with a great pair of tongs in his hand. Now this smith was a merry fellow, full of tricks and pranks.

When the smith saw them hobbling and limping along, he laughed so that he was almost bent in two. Then he bawled out, "Surely this is a new flock of geese the Princess is going to have. Who can tell which is goose and which is gander? This must be the gander that toddles in front. Goosey! Goosey! Goosey!" he called out. With that he threw his hands about as though he were scattering corn for the geese.

But the flock never stopped. On it went. All that the goody and the man did was to look daggers at the smith for making game of them.

Then the smith, who was a stout, strong fellow, thought it would be fine fun to see if he could hold the whole flock.

With his big tongs he took hold of the old man's coattail. The man all the while bellowed and wriggled, but Taper Tom only said, "Hang on, if you care to come with us."

So the smith had to go along too. He bent his back and stuck his heels into the hill and tried to get loose. But it was all no good. He stuck fast. Whether he wanted to or not, he had to dance along with the rest.

When they came to the King's palace, a dog ran out and began to bark as though they were wolves or beggars. The Princess looked out of the window to see what was the matter. When she set eyes on this strange pack, she laughed quietly to herself. But Taper Tom was not content with that.

"Wait a bit," he said. "She'll soon have to open her mouth wider." And he turned off with his band to the back of the palace.

When they passed by the kitchen, the door stood open. The cook was just beating the porridge. But when she saw Taper Tom and his pack, she came running out the door with her whisk in one hand and a ladle full of smoking porridge in the other. She laughed as though her sides would split. And when she saw the smith there, too, she began laughing again in a loud peal. But when she had tired of laughing, she also thought the golden goose so lovely that she must stroke it.

"Taper Tom! Taper Tom!" she called out, and came running with the ladle of porridge. "May I stroke that pretty goose of yours?"

"Better let her stroke me," said the smith.

When the cook heard that, she got angry.

"What is that you say?" she cried, and let fly at the smith with the ladle.

"Hang on, if you care to come with us," said Taper Tom.

So she, too, stuck fast. For all her kicks and plunges and all her scolding and screaming, she, too, had to limp along with the others.

Soon they all came to the window of the Princess. There she stood, waiting for them. When she saw they had taken the cook, too, ladle and all, she opened her mouth wide. She laughed so loud that the King had to hold her up.

So Taper Tom got the Princess and half the kingdom. And they had such a merry wedding, it was heard and talked of far and wide.

Why the Bear Is Stumpy-tailed

ONE DAY A BEAR met a fox who came slinking along with a string of fish he had stolen.

"That's a fine catch of fish you have there," said the bear. "Where did you get them?"

"Oh, My Lord Bruin, I've been out fishing and caught them," said the fox.

So the bear, who was very fond of fish, wanted to learn to fish, too. He asked the fox to tell him how to set about it.

"Oh, it's easy for you," answered the fox, "and very soon learned. You have only to go upon the ice, cut a hole right through, and stick your tail down into it. You must hold it there as long as you can. Don't mind if your tail smarts a little— that's when the fish bite, and sometimes they bite a bit hard. The longer you hold it there, the more fish you will get. Then all at once, pull it out, with a cross pull sideways—and a strong pull, too."

The bear did as the fox said. He cut a hole right through the ice and sat there. He kept his tail down in the hole through the ice for a long, long time. The more his tail smarted, the more he thought of what a fine lot of fish he was catching.

When the bear thought he had caught enough,

his tail was fast frozen in the ice. He gave it a strong pull, with a cross pull sideways, too—and it snapped right off.

That is why to this very day Bruin the bear goes about with a stumpy tail.

The Lad and the North Wind

ONCE UPON A TIME there was an old widow who had one son. Since she was ill and weak, she asked her son to go into their little storehouse to get some porridge meal for cooking. As he came out of the storehouse and was going down the steps, he met the North

Wind, puffing and blowing. A great blast caught up the meal, and carried it off through the air.

The lad went back into the storehouse for more meal. When he came out again on the steps, the North Wind blew at him a second time and carried off the meal with a great puff.

More than that—the North Wind did so a third time.

At this the lad got very angry. Since it seemed all wrong that the North Wind should behave this way, he decided to go find the North Wind and ask for the meal back.

Off the lad went. The way was long, and he walked and walked. But at last he came to the North Wind's house.

"Good day!" said the lad. "And thank you for coming to see us yesterday."

"GOOD DAY!" answered the North Wind, in a voice that was loud and gruff. "AND THANKS FOR COMING TO SEE ME. WHAT DO YOU WANT?"

"Oh," answered the lad. "I only wished to ask you to please let me have back the meal that you took from me. We haven't much to live on. If you're going to go on snapping up the little we have, there will be nothing for me and my poor old mother to do but to starve."

"I DO NOT HAVE YOUR MEAL," said the North Wind. "BUT, IF YOU ARE IN SUCH NEED, I'LL GIVE YOU A TABLECLOTH WHICH WILL GET YOU EVERYTHING YOU WANT. IF YOU ONLY SAY, 'CLOTH, SPREAD YOURSELF,' IT WILL SERVE UP ALL KINDS OF GOOD DISHES."

With this the lad was well content. But, as the way was long, he couldn't get home in one day.

He stopped at an inn on the way. When they were going to sit down to supper, he laid the cloth on a table which stood in the corner and said, "Cloth, spread yourself, and serve up all kinds of good dishes."

He had scarcely said this before the cloth did

as it was bid. All who stood by thought it a fine thing, but the landlord most of all.

When everyone was fast asleep that night, the landlord took the lad's cloth, and put another like it in its place. But this cloth could not serve up so much as a crumb of dry bread.

When the lad awoke, he picked up his cloth and went off with it. That same day he got home to his mother.

"Now," he said, "I've been to the North Wind's house. I have seen what a good fellow he is, for he gave me this cloth. When I say to it, 'Cloth, spread yourself, and serve up all kinds of good dishes,' I get any sort of food I please."

"All very true, I daresay," said his mother. "But seeing is believing. I shall not believe it until I see it."

The lad made haste, drew out a table, laid the cloth on it, and said, "Cloth, spread yourself, and serve up all kinds of good dishes."

Not a bit of dry bread did the cloth serve up!

"Well," said the lad. "There's no help for it.
I must go to the North Wind again."

And away he went.

Late in the afternoon he came to the North
Wind's house.

"Good evening!" said the lad.

"GOOD EVENING!" answered the North Wind.

"I want my rights for that meal you took," said the lad. "As for that cloth you gave me, it isn't worth a penny."

"I DO NOT HAVE YOUR MEAL," said the North Wind. "BUT YOU MAY HAVE THAT RAM OVER THERE. IT WILL MAKE GOLD PIECES AS SOON AS YOU SAY, 'RAM, RAM! MAKE MONEY!'"

Well, the lad thought this a fine thing. But, as it was too far to get home that day, he stopped for the night at the same inn where he had slept the last time.

Before he called for supper, he decided to see if what the North Wind had said about the ram was true, and he found that it was.

Now the landlord also saw what the ram gave, and he thought it was indeed a marvelous animal. When the lad had fallen asleep, he took another ram which could not make gold pieces, and switched the two.

Next morning, off went the lad. When he got home to his mother, he said, "After all, the North Wind is a jolly fellow. Now he has given me a ram which can make gold pieces if I only say, 'Ram, ram! Make money!'"

"All very true, I daresay," said his mother. "But I shall not believe any such thing until I see the gold pieces made."

"Ram, ram! Make money!" said the lad. But not one piece did the ram give.

The lad went back again to the North Wind, and he called to him in anger. He said the ram was worth nothing, and he must have his rights for the meal.

"WELL," said the North Wind, "I HAVE NOTH-ING ELSE TO GIVE YOU BUT THAT OLD STICK IN THE CORNER. WITH THIS, IF YOU SAY, 'STICK, STICK! LAY ON!' IT BEATS UNTIL YOU SAY, 'STICK, STICK! NOW STOP!'"

Well, the lad thanked the North Wind for the stick and went on home.

Since the way was long, he spent this night, once again, at the inn. He could pretty well guess what had happened to the cloth and the ram, so he lay down at once on the bench and began to snore as if he were asleep.

Now the landlord, who had easily seen that the stick must be something special, hunted up another one which looked like it. As soon as he heard the lad snoring, he went to exchange the two. He was about to take it, when the lad shouted out, "Stick, stick! Lay on!"

The stick beat the landlord till he jumped over chairs and tables and benches and yelled and roared, "Oh my! Oh my! Beg the stick to stop, or it will beat me to death. You shall have back both your cloth and your ram."

When the lad thought the landlord had been beaten enough, he said, "Stick, stick! Now stop!"

He then took up the cloth and put it into his pocket. He went home with his stick in his hand, leading the ram by a cord tied around its horns. And so it was he got his rights for the meal he had lost.

Boots and the Troll

ONCE UPON A TIME a poor man had three sons. When he died, the two older sons set off into the world to try their luck. They would not at any price take the youngest with them. They despised him and called him Boots and made him do the dirty work.

The two went off and got work at a palace—one under the coachman, the other under the gardener. Boots set off, too, and took with him a great kneading trough. This large wooden bread maker was the only thing his parents had left their sons. The two older brothers would not bother with it. Though it was heavy to carry, Boots did not want to leave it behind.

After he had walked a bit, Boots came to the palace and asked for work. They said they did not need him, but Boots begged so prettily that at last he got a place in the kitchen. He was to carry in wood and water for the cook.

Being quick and ready, Boots soon made everyone like him. His two brothers were so slow that they received more kicks than pennies. They envied Boots when they saw how much better he did than they.

Now just opposite the palace, across a lake, lived a Troll. He had seven silver ducks which swam on the lake and could be seen from the palace. The King had often longed for them.

The two older brothers said to the coachman one day, "If our brother only chose, he could easily get the King those seven silver ducks."

It wasn't long before the coachman repeated this to the King. The King called Boots before him and ordered, "Your brothers say you can get me the silver ducks. Go now and fetch them."

"But I'm sure I never thought or said anything of the kind," answered Boots.

"You did say so, and you shall fetch them," insisted the King.

"Well, well," said the lad. "I suppose I must. Give me a bushel of rye and a bushel of wheat, and I'll see what I can do."

He took the rye and the wheat and put them into the kneading trough he had brought with him from home. Next he climbed in himself and rowed across the lake. On the other side, he began to walk along the shore, throwing out the grain until at last he coaxed the ducks into his kneading trough. Then he rowed back as fast as ever he could.

When Boots was halfway over, the Troll came out of his house and saw him.

"Hallo!" roared out the Troll. "Is it you that has gone off with my seven silver ducks?"

"Aye, aye!" said the lad.

"Shall you be back soon?" asked the Troll.

"Very likely," said the lad.

When he got to the King with the seven ducks, Boots was more popular than ever. Even the King was pleased to say, "Well done!"

★ ★ ★

Boots saw his brothers growing more and more spiteful and envious. They told the coachman that their brother had said he was man enough to get the King the Troll's bed quilt. This fine spread was put together with a gold patch and a silver patch, then a silver patch and a gold patch.

Again the coachman repeated all this to the King. The King told the lad what his brothers had said, that he was clever enough to steal the Troll's bed quilt with its gold and silver patches. Now he must do it, or lose his life.

Boots answered that he had never thought or said any such thing. But when he found there was no help for it, he begged for time to think about it.

When three days were gone, Boots again rowed across the lake in his kneading trough and went spying about. At last he saw servants come out of the Troll's cave and hang the quilt out to air.

As soon as they had gone back into the cave, Boots pulled the quilt down and rowed away with it as fast as he could.

When Boots was halfway across, out came the Troll. He saw Boots and roared, "Hallo! Is it you who took my seven silver ducks?"

"Aye, aye!" said the lad.

"And now, have you taken my bed quilt, with the silver patches and gold patches, and gold patches and silver patches?"

"Aye, aye!" said the lad.

"Shall you come back again?"

"Very likely," said the lad.

When he returned to the palace with the gold and silver patchwork quilt, everyone seemed fonder of him than ever. He was promoted to the King's body servant.

At this, the other two brothers were still more angry. They went and told the coachman, "Now our brother has said he is man enough to get the Troll's gold harp. That harp has such magic in it that all who listen to it grow glad, however sad they may have been."

Once more the coachman went to the King. And the King said to Boots, "If you have said this, you shall do it. If you do it, you shall have the Princess and half the kingdom. If you don't, you shall lose your life."

"I'm sure I never thought or said anything of the kind," answered Boots. "But if there's no help for it, I may as well try. I must have six days to think about it."

Yes, he might have six days, but when they were over, he must set out.

★ ★ ★

Boots put a tenpenny nail, a wooden pin, and a wax candle end in his pocket. He rowed across the lake and walked up and down before the Troll's cave, looking stealthily about him. When the Troll came out, he saw Boots at once.

"Ho, ho!" roared the Troll. "Is it you who took my seven silver ducks?"

"Aye, aye!" said the lad.

"And is it you who took my bed quilt with the gold and silver patches?" asked the Troll.

"Aye, aye!" said the lad.

The Troll caught hold of Boots at once, and took him into his cave.

"Daughter dear," said the Troll, "I've caught the fellow who stole my silver ducks and my bed quilt with gold and silver patches. Put him into the fattening coop. When he's fat, we'll kill him and make a feast for our friends."

She was willing enough, and put him at once into the fattening coop. There he stayed eight days. He fed on the best, both in meat and drink, and as much of each as he could cram. When the eight days were over, the Troll told his daughter to go down and cut into the lad's little finger, so that they might see if he were fat. Down she went to the coop.

"Out with your little finger," she said.

But Boots stuck out his tenpenny nail, and she cut at it.

"Nay, nay! He's as hard as iron still," said the

Troll's daughter, when she got back to her father. "We can't take him yet."

Eight days later the same thing happened. This time Boots stuck out his wooden pin.

"Well, he's a little better," she said, when she got back to the Troll. "But he'll still be as hard as wood to chew."

When another eight days were gone, the Troll told his daughter to go down and see if he wasn't fat now.

"Out with your little finger," said the Troll's daughter when she reached the coop. This time Boots stuck out the candle end.

"Now he'll do nicely," she said.

"Will he?" said the Troll. "Well then, I'll just set off and invite the guests. Meantime you must kill him, and roast half and boil half."

When the Troll had been gone a little while, the daughter began to sharpen a great long knife.

"Is that what you're going to kill me with?" asked the lad.

"Yes, it is," said she.

"But it isn't sharp," said the lad. "Just let me sharpen it for you, and then you'll find it easier work to kill me."

So she let him have the knife, and he began to rub and sharpen it.

"Just let me try it on one of your braids. I think it's about right now."

She let him do that. But he grasped the braid of hair, pulled back her head and in one stroke cut it off. Half of her he then roasted, and half of her he boiled, and he served it all up.

After that Boots dressed himself in her clothes and hid in the corner.

When the Troll came home with his guests, he called out to his daughter to come and eat a bit.

"No, thank you," said the lad. "I don't care for food. I'm so sad and downcast."

"Oh," said the Troll, "if that's all, you know the cure. Take the harp and play a tune on it."

"Yes," said the lad, "but where has it gone? I can't find it."

"Why, you know well enough," said the Troll. "You used it last. Where should it be but above the door?"

The lad did not wait to be told twice. He took down the harp and went in and out playing tunes. Then all at once, he shoved off the kneading trough, jumped in, and rowed away so fast that the foam flew around him.

After a while the Troll thought his daughter had been gone a long time, so he went out to see what ailed her. He saw the lad in the trough, far, far out on the lake. "Hallo!" he roared. "Is it you that took my seven silver ducks?"

"Aye, aye!" said the lad.

"Is it you that took my bed quilt with the gold and silver patches?"

"Yes!" said the lad.

"And now you have taken off with my gold harp?" screamed the Troll.

"Yes," said the lad. "I've got it, sure enough."

"And haven't I eaten you up after all, then?"

"No, no! It was your own daughter you ate," answered the lad.

When the Troll heard that, he was so angry he burst.

Boots then rowed secretly back to the cave and carried away as many of the Troll's gold and silver pieces as his trough could hold.

When he presented the gold harp to the King, Boots received in turn the Princess and half the kingdom, as the King had promised. As for the brothers, Boots treated them well, for he thought they had only wished him good in what they had said.

About This Series

IN RECENT DECADES, folk tales and fairy tales from all corners of the earth have been made available in a variety of handsome collections and in lavishly illustrated picture books. But in the 1950s, such a rich selection was not yet available. The classic fairy and folk tales were most often found in cumbersome books with small print and few illustrations. Helen Jones, then children's book editor at Little, Brown and Company, accepted a proposal from a Boston librarian for an ambitious series with a simple goal — to put an international selection of stories into the hands of children. The tales would be published in slim volumes, with wide margins and ample leading, and illustrated by a cast of contemporary artists. The result was a unique series of books intended for children to read by themselves — the Favorite Fairy Tales series. Available only in hardcover for many years, the books have now been reissued in paperbacks that feature new illustrations and covers.

The series embraces the stories of sixteen different

countries: France, England, Germany, India, Ireland, Sweden, Poland, Russia, Spain, Czechoslovakia, Scotland, Denmark, Japan, Greece, Italy, and Norway. Some of these stories may seem violent or fantastical to our modern sensibilities, yet they often reflect the deepest yearnings and imaginings of the human mind and heart.

Virginia Haviland traveled abroad frequently and was able to draw upon librarians, storytellers, and writers in countries as far away as Japan to help make her selections. But she was also an avid researcher with a keen interest in rare books, and most of the stories she included in the series were found through a diligent search of old collections. Ms. Haviland was associated with the Boston Public Library for nearly thirty years—as a children's and branch librarian, and eventually as Readers Advisor to Children. She reviewed for *The Horn Book Magazine* for almost thirty years and in 1963 was named Head of the Children's Book Section of the Library of Congress. Ms. Haviland remained with the Library of Congress for nearly twenty years and wrote and lectured about children's literature throughout her career. She died in 1988.